J.E. STAMPER

UGLY
ME

I greatly appreciate you taking the time to read my book.
Please consider leaving a review wherever you bought the book
and telling your friends about it.

Thank you so much for your support.

Before you read <u>Ugly Me</u>, check out the free prequel story!

Visit the link below to receive a free eBook and audiobook version!

https://www.jestamper.com/sign-up

For Jessie, the love of my life.

With you, I am blessed, amazed, complete.

Foreword

THOUGH THIS BOOK is a work of fiction, it was born, as I expect most fiction truly is, from a very real place in my life.

I'd always wanted to be a writer. I'd had countless dreams of serene hours spent in contemplative inspiration at a grand antique writing desk in a sunny nook overlooking a grandiose landscape. In those fantasies, I'd sip hot tea and pen bestsellers in my pajamas while my family enjoyed a comfortable life, living on royalties and sunshine and giant doses of quiet contentment.

But after years of waiting around for the "right moment," shopping around for the best writing software, scouring the web for the most pretentious-looking notebooks and fancy pens, all the while actually writing next-to-nothing, I finally realized something.

I wanted to *be* a writer, but I was not willing to do what it took to *become* a writer. I wanted to *have done* all those incredible things, but I lacked the drive to actually get off my butt and try to *do* them. I had a clear picture of what I wanted, but I was too afraid to actually begin.

That's really what it was. Fear.

And it took a bunch of schoolchildren to help me get over this fear and actually start doing something.

You see, after years spent working in public education, both as a teacher and an administrator, I had entered a dark place. Emotionally exhausted, mentally stressed, discouraged, and defeated, I was teetering on the edge of despair. I was sick of seeing so many people put each other through so much hell for no reason at all (I'm talking about children and adults alike), and I felt helpless to stop it.

But seeing so many children leave to broken homes full of neglect and abuse only to return day after day and give living another shot inspired me and gave me the courage I needed to quit making fear-filled excuses. I wanted to tell their stories. I wanted to give these invisible sufferers a voice and, with it, hope for a brighter future.

So I wrote.

I poured my heart out. I didn't have the fancy writing nook or the luxury of a full-time writing schedule, but I did have a purpose. In the darkness of my dining room, as my beautiful wife and children slept and (hopefully) dreamed pleasant dreams, I wrote.

Night after night.

Until I was done.

For the first time in my life.

And you're now holding that book in your hands.

I don't expect to be a bestseller or to gain any amount of riches or fame from this little book, but I do wholeheartedly hope that the folks who read it will see the people around them with more understanding and treat them with more compassion. I hope that my paltry words will somehow make the world a better place.

Now, read this book and go make someone's life a little happier.

Chapter 1

THE ALARM ON my phone cuts through the thing I call sleep now. I sit up on the sofa and stare at the broken screen. It's the first day of seventh grade. Mom is in the bed by the window, drooling into her dingy pillowcase. She slept right through the alarm, dead to the world.

Shane was over again last night, so she's probably strung out again. Chances are, she'll still be in bed when I get back from school.

I pull on shoes that are too tight, a shirt that is too big, and jeans that have too many holes. I look for a PopTart in the kitchen, but I can't find one. Mom probably hid them again so she would have something to eat when she wakes up. I've gotten pretty good at finding the food she hides and at taking the crap she gives me when she finds out I've eaten her stash, but I hear the rumble of the bus down the street. Thankfully, after a summer full of PopTart hunts, I have better things to do.

At least I'll get to eat at school. Spoiled kids complain about the school food and whine because the fries are soggy and say that the stuff looks like barf and tastes like crap. But I've gotten good at pretending to hate the food while simultaneously eating everything I can. Most days after lunch, I make excuses to my friends, telling them I have to go to the bathroom or something. But really I'm going back to the cafeteria, stuffing my backpack with the school lunch rejects, small plastic bags of carrots and apple slices left behind by kids too cool to be seen eating something that doesn't have a flashy label.

The janitor lady sees me, but she doesn't say anything. Sometimes she gathers the leftovers in a neat little pile for me.

The bus appears over the top of the hill. In the glare of the headlights, I see a smiling mom down the street taking pictures of her son in his new school clothes with his new backpack and his new lunchbox. He has black slicked-back hair. She wipes tears away from her eyes. "I can't believe you're in middle school now!" she says.

That's nice. At least she dragged her ass out of bed for him.

I can't believe there's a kid who lives this close to me that I've never met. But then again, his mom probably doesn't want him hanging out with kids like me.

Kids like me.

Kids who curse and fight and wear dirty, smelly, worn-out clothes. The kind of kids you see on the street and shake your head and say, "Look at what the world's coming to." The kind of kids who float through life like so much pollution. The kids you see and wonder where the hell the parents are but don't bother to stop and ask. The detention/suspension/juvie throwaways who leave a bad taste in everyone's mouths.

Kids like me.

I can't say I blame her.

The bus makes its way to my house, coughs, wheezes, and opens its doors. They squeak. As I approach the bus, I tell myself that this year will be better than the last, that this year will be different. I try to channel all that new-age Oprah vision board positivity stuff and fool myself into thinking that this will be the year that it all comes together.

Because this is the year that I finally find a way to beat the monster, the Ugly Me who lives inside. The Ugly Me who lurks, just beneath the surface, waiting to lash out. The Ugly Me who feeds on pain and tears and belches out anger and hurt.

But as my foot hits the rubberized tread of the bus steps, my heart begins to race, and I seriously think about turning around and running back into my house, shutting myself in where, sure, I'll have to find a way to get some breakfast, but at least I won't have to put up with all those disgusted faces and rolling eyes and hurting words and...

I dash onto the bus and find a seat without making eye contact with anyone. So far so good.

The bus smells like it always does. Like a bus. There's really nothing to compare it to. Anyone who's ever been on a school bus in the past however-long-there's-been-school-buses knows exactly what I'm talking about. They could bottle that smell up and use it as a kid repellent.

The bus stops again and this high school kid gets on. He sits down heavy next to me and I scooch over and squash myself against the window, hoping to just melt into it and slide down to the floor.

His name is Drake or Blake or something and he smells like he used about a half a can of that body spray that all the boys are always spraying on themselves these days. They think it will make women fall all over them like in the YouTube ads, but really it smells like puke took a dump on some garbage and put it in an aerosol can and sold it to a stupid, gullible teenage boy.

"Hey, Matilda," he says.

"Hey," I mumble back. I feel super awkward because the last time I saw him, my mom called his mom a bitch and said she would beat the crap out of her if she looked at her like that again. I felt really bad for the lady. All she did was walk by our house and wave, but Mom was in a mood. And when Mom is in a mood, well, she gets like that.

"How's it going?" he asks. I turn my head a little bit. His jeans are dirty. Not just normal dirty, but more like these-are-my-only-jeans dirty.

"It's Miranda," I say. "And I'm okay, I guess. For the first day of school, anyway."

"Eighth grade?"

"Seventh grade."

"Ouch," he says. "Seventh grade was the worst year of my life. I'm talking *bad*. And I'm starting tenth grade for the second time this year. That's how bad it was."

Well, that makes me feel just dandy.

The bus bumps on, and by the time my school comes into

sight, I'm shaking in my seat.

Chapter 2

THE PRINCIPAL, MR. Gorley, stands outside, propping the door open with his foot. He has this big, goofy smile on his face. He greets us as we come in and gives us high fives and fist bumps. He asks some kids how their summers were.

He doesn't ask me. He probably knows that mine was a real shitshow and that I really don't want to talk about it, nope, not one teeny bit. I just want to get to the cafeteria, grab some breakfast, and find a dark corner to hide in.

"Good to see you, Miranda," he says.

"Thanks," I say, not stopping to talk more because I'm riding the wave of preteens through the door and up the huge staircase.

It is actually good to see him, too. For a principal, he's not a bad guy. He smiles a lot and seems to really like kids. I don't know what he's smoking, but he must be on some good stuff to keep putting up with all the crazy crap that happens around here.

And he doesn't yell at me like pretty much everyone else, even when I really screw up.

No one talks to me as I head up the hallway to the cafeteria. So far, so good. If no one talks to me, then at least they can't say anything about my stringy hair or my dirty thrift store reject clothes.

I step into the cafeteria, already crowded with kids. I feel my heart pounding like a machine gun in my chest as I scan the room, looking for a friendly face within the sea of students. What I see are tons of kids, chatting it up, smiling, trading summer stories, showing off their fresh department store looks.

5

How can they all look so happy? How can they all seem like they belong here? Like they were 3D printed from some middle school molding machine. Why, when I look around the room with like 200 kids, can't I find any other kids like me?

"Have a seat!" some lady teacher yells from across the cafeteria. I flinch like I've been slapped and kind of come to like I'm snapping out of a trance or something. I've been standing there in the middle of the cafeteria just looking around like an idiot, totally frozen. Other people start to notice me. Kids are giving me those "What the hell is her problem?" looks.

What an idiot.

I bolt over to the serving line and snatch up a styrofoam tray and squeeze it to my chest with both arms. I feel the squeaky crack of the styrofoam and realize I'm squeezing too hard. I'm hustled through the line and handed a milk, some kind of weird blue juice, a carton of fruit loops, and a banana.

"Dollar twenty-five," says the lady at the cash register. I don't recognize her, but her name tag tells me that her name is Sasha. She looks too young to be a lunch lady.

"Oh, I...um," I say as I rummage around in my pockets, doing the "I know I've got the money somewhere because I'm not really a broke-ass loser with a drug addict mom at home who never gives me money for anything because she spends every cent she gets on dope and stupid crap" routine.

Miss Ruthie, the old lunch lady dishing out bananas, sees what's going on and clears her throat and gives the new lady a sideways kind of look. "It's okay honey," Miss Ruthie says. "You just take your breakfast and go on, now."

Let's just say that Miss Ruthie and I go way back.

I turn and head back into the cafeteria with my loaded tray. I take one tiny step into the cafeteria, and my tray gives up the ghost. It folds itself forward and dumps its contents onto the floor. My milk explodes like a cold, wet grenade and douses my shoes.

The commotion wasn't that bad compared to the general insanity of a middle school cafeteria, but several people notice and start staring at me. A few people laugh, and one joker starts to applaud.

Before I know it, the whole cafeteria is applauding. Most of them don't know why, but middle schoolers are like sheep. One idiot does something stupid, and everyone else follows along without really knowing why. Without really knowing how it feels to be on the losing side of their mindless complicity.

Without knowing or without caring?

I dump the rest of my tray and jet out of the cafeteria, a high-volume "Get back here and clean that up right now, young lady!" following closely behind. I ignore the command and hightail it into the bathroom.

I honestly feel bad about the mess that Miss Kate, the nice janitor lady, will have to clean up. Not a good start to her school year, either.

I land in the center stall and slam the door. It seems that I've gained some kind of weird superpower-y embarrassment-fueled strength because the door ricochets and jams me in the bony knee. Hot, angry pain throbs through my leg, and I bite down on my wrist to keep from screaming in pain.

I finally get the door closed and locked and plop myself down onto the toilet. Elbows on my knees, my face cupped in my hands, I fight back tears and rock back and forth.

How could I have thought that this year would be any different? A kid like me doesn't belong here.

Chapter 3

WHILE I'M IN here throwing my little pity party, some girl is pooping in the stall next to me. I mean *pooping* pooping. Like, really going for it. It's as if that poor toilet insulted her mother or something and she's trying to teach the thing a lesson. It's like Plop City in here as she just goes to town.

And the smell! I've never accused a school bathroom of smelling good even on the best of days, but I think she's peeling the paint off the walls. Pretty soon I'll be able to see last year's graffiti.

I try to let my misery chase away the smile forming on my lips, but the sounds and the smells are just too strong. I start to giggle. I smash my lips together to keep it in, but the laughter escapes through my nose and eventually takes over.

"Oh my God!" I say, struggling to breathe, "Are you ok in there?"

"Yeah, yeah. Laugh it up," replies a voice. It's as flat as roadkill, no emotion whatsoever.

"Sorry," I say, still giggling.

"S'alright," replies the voice, "Stupid IBS flaring up. *Nervous I guess.*" The last sentence was spoken through the filter of a strained grunt. "Slammed that door over there awfully hard. Thought you were going to tear the place down."

"Sorry," I say again.

"And judging from the fact that your pants aren't around your ankles right now, I'd say that you didn't come in here to see to your biological urgencies."

"Huh?"

"You didn't run in here like a preteen tornado just to take a leak. You came in here under great emotional duress." Not wanting to admit that she was right, I let a moment of silence creep into the conversation.

"Your silence speaks volumes, sister," she says, "so spill it. What's up?"

I don't know if it's the fact that I can't see her and don't recognize her voice as that of an enemy or if the whole situation is just that absurd or if it's something about her weird way of talking, but I actually find myself feeling like talking to the mystery pooper. Go figure.

"I don't know," I begin, "It's stupid, really. I came here thinking that things would be different this year. Thinking that somehow summer would've changed everything and people would've suddenly decided to not be a bunch of jerk nuggets. Was pretty excited to come here today, actually. If you can believe it."

I hear a deep, overly sympathetic sigh from the other side of the wall. "And I would venture to guess that something has already happened to bring these foolish expectations crashing to the ground?"

"You got it," I reply.

"And what force of adolescence shattered your world today?" she asks. "What apocalyptic occurrence has brought you into the porcelain refuge?"

I'm tempted to feel like she's totally being a sarcastic snot right now, but she's somehow pulling this conversation off. She's got a good way of talking: grown up, but not so grown up that it makes me feel like she's talking down to me.

"I froze up in the cafeteria. Stood there staring at all the kids in there like a complete idiot, got yelled at by some teacher, totally dropped everything and doused my shoes with milk. Then some jerk started to clap and everyone joined in."

"Ouch," she says. "Rough start, all right. Nothing like being the unwilling the center of attention." She pauses for a second. "I've got you beat, though."

"What do you mean?" I ask.

"Last year at my old school, I pooped my pants in front of my entire gym class."

"Nun-uh," I say, in stunned denial of such an outrageous confession. I mean, we're in middle school, a world filled with vicious, immature hyenas just waiting to pounce at the slightest whiff of distress. Something like that would be nothing short of social suicide.

"Yup," she says. "We were running laps, and I felt a rumble, you know, thought I just needed to release a bit of gastrointestinal air pressure."

"Oh God," I say, knowing where this story was heading, laughter beginning to filter into my voice.

"Yeah," she continues, "Thought I was safe to just crop dust a little bit and continue on my merry way, so--"

"Crop dust?" I interrupt.

"You know," she says in a how-the-hell-do-you-not-know-this tone, "When you have to fart but you're walking around in a crowded place so you just kind of do a slow release as you walk along so it just kind of blends in to everything."

"Oh. Gotcha. I've done that tons of times."

"Right? Anyway, turns out there was, *ahem*, more to the story, and I left a trail from the gym all the way to the bathroom. They had to evacuate the gym while the janitor came in with some special disinfectant and cleaned the whole gym floor."

"You're right," I say, sympathetic horror shutting down my laughter.

"About what?"

"You've got me beat."

"Told you so," she says.

"So what happened? Did you have to change schools? I mean, if that happened to me, I think I might just catch the next train out of town and commit myself to the life of a middle school hobo."

"To be honest, sitting there in that bathroom with my defiled undies, trying to clean myself up with the last four squares of a roll of woefully thin toilet paper, I thought my life was over. I thought that there was no way a girl who just took a dump in the gym could ever hope to have a normal life."

"Did people make fun of you?" I ask.

"Absolutely," she says with a chuckle. "And I got called lots of names. And people gave me grossed-out looks. And people laughed at me when they walked by. You know how kids our age are."

"Yep," I say, thinking about the sea of sarcastic applause that I had just swam through to get where I am now.

"And I begged my parents to let me change schools, pleaded, cried, tore my clothes, covered myself in ashes, fully participated in every dramatic gesture I'd ever heard of. But no dice. I had to go back, day after day."

"I'm so sorry. That must've been horrible," I say. "So how did you deal?"

The sound of the morning bell cuts through the still-putrid air, interrupting our little chat.

"Guess that's a story for another time," she says. She nudges my dingy, milk-soaked sneaker with hers (a brand-new pair of Nikes). "Now go on, Miss Dairy, don't want to add tardiness to your list of first-day complications."

Chapter 4

FIRST PERIOD IS Mr. Worsham's life science class. He's this old guy with a wicked combover and one of those TV teacher jackets with the patches on the elbows. His voice is all nasal-y and he gives off a major Mr. Rogers vibe. His voice disappears into the background of my mind as I picture him going home and changing into slippers and a cardigan and singing songs about how sharing is caring and a bunch of other touchy-feely bullcrap like that.

And suddenly I'm back there. I'm back there and Dad's there and I'm so small and I can smell him and I can hear Mom screaming in the other room and he's yelling loud, loud, loud like the whole house is about to fall down and I'm staring at the cracked TV screen watching that same old DVD for the thousandth time like a good little girl but I can't hear the ding-ding of the trolley taking all us kids into the Neighborhood of Make-Believe because he's so loud and I just want to disappear into the wall with that little red car because I want to be anywhere but here and Mom is screaming and crying but if I sit here like a good little girl and pretend like we're the perfect little TV family then he'll leave me alone but I'm stuck and she's stuck and--

"Young lady!" shouts Mr. Worsham. The world swirls back into focus, and I wonder how long he's been trying to get my attention because he's a little red in the face and his combover has gone crooked.

The splash sends ripples of nervous giggles around the room. I wipe some wet from the corner of my eye, hoping no one notices.

"Can you pass those back, please?" he asks, pointing toward a stack of papers on my desk. I hand them back without bothering to look at them, and he leans a bit closer and says in one of those fake pretending-to-whisper-but-not-really-whispering voices, "Do you need to go see the nurse?"

I think about that for a second. Not unless she can de-milkify my shoes or shake me up like an Etch-a-Sketch and reset my life or change my stupid ugly face or give me a lobotomy or fix my frizzy hair.

"Nope," I say instead, "I'm ok."

"Then if you can't pay attention you can just take yourself down to the office," he says in a very un-Mister Rogers voice.

I'm tempted to take him up on the offer because, like most people, he obviously doesn't want me around. I decide to stick around, though. "I'm sorry," I say.

He nods this curt little nod and walks away, droning on about how important it is to learn about the living world around us and how that we're going to do a ton of really fun things like dissect baby pigs and learn to grow our own food. Sounds like it's going to be another big fat trip Boringville to me. He says that life is nothing short of amazing and that we don't have to look very far to witness miracles. He makes a big show of pointing out the window. I roll my eyes and follow his hand.

"What do you see?" he asks in a super-dramatic, slightly hushed tone. I'll bet he was in front of the mirror last night practicing this little routine.

I get where he's going with this. He wants us to look out and see the miraculous wonders of Mother Nature. He wants us to go all zen or whatever and ponder the meaning of existence or some crap like that. But we're a bunch of seventh-grade sacks full of crazy and hormones. Good luck getting any of us to ponder anything beyond our phone screens.

What do I see?

I look beyond the trees and grass that he's so clearly wanting us to go ga-ga over to this place in the distance. It's this big, new shopping center the size of a small town, and in it I see shiny new signs for a bunch of shiny new shops where people can buy shiny new things.

I hoofed it up there back in July just to check it out. It's a hell of a walk, so by the time I got there I was sweating my butt off. Like, seriously stanky dripping. I walked into this hip clothing store, and the checkout lady took one look at me and said something into her geeky little headset microphone. Before I could take two steps, this burly guy came out from some back room and stuck to me tighter than my sweaty shorts. I tried to smile at him in that "I may look like a street rat thief, but I really just wanted to look around and feel normal for a freakin' second" type of way, but he was all frowny-face just waiting for me to lift something so he'd have an excuse to release some pent-up testosterone rage on me.

I left and walked back home. I felt like an idiot for even thinking that I could dip a toe into the world outside of my own little corner of Crazytown.

I'm still staring out the window long after the rest of the class is back to pretending to pay attention to Science Teacher Man. When I decide to tune back in, he's off on some tangent about grizzly bears. I hear a couple of girls behind me whispering and giggling. When I turn around, they lock eyes with me and go back to whispering. I just know they're talking about me. They're dressed like they just jumped off the pages of a fashion magazine. Stupid stuck-up preps.

I blast them with the old one finger salute and turn around before I can see the looks on their stupid too-much-makeup-wearing faces.

I turn my attention back to Mr. Worsham. That combover, though. I spend the rest of the period praying for a rogue gust of wind to come along and make it dance.

Chapter 5

THE BELL LIBERATES me from torture-by-science, and I scoot into the hallway. It's time for math class with Ms. Odum. If the graffiti on the gym wall is to be believed, she's this menopausal mess with a sharp tongue and an attitude from Hell.

This should be fun.

When I get to her door I can see her sitting at this enormous desk completely absorbed in whatever's on her computer screen. Probably checking the balance on her retirement account and calculating exactly how many more days she'll have to show her face here before she can check out. I try to slide through the door all ninja-style and take a seat in the back.

"Nuh-uh!" she yells. I just about jump out of my freakin' skin. "I've heard about you, Missy," she says and narrows her eyes at me as she peeks over her computer screen. "Front seat!" she yells again and snaps her finger at a desk in the front row.

She glares at me. I'm talking real eye daggers, here. Meanwhile, my blood begins to boil, and I feel myself stiffen. I start to breathe hard, and I clench my fists into bony little lumps. It's on. I turn on my laser vision and stare right back.

"Why?" I ask, not trying to hide the total pissedoffness in my voice.

"Because I had a little conversation with Ms. Bell and she told me all about you and your little attitude problem. I've got my eye on you, young lady," she replies, her voice dripping hot hatred. "Now sit!"

I stand there, eyes locked with hers. So this witch thinks she

15

knows me just because she had a little chat with the hens in the teacher's lounge? I feel Ugly Me scratching beneath the surface, begging to come out and devour this so-called teacher lady.

Other students start to filter in. A couple of oblivious knotheads just come in and pick seats as if there's not an epic student-teacher bloodbath brewing. But most of the other kids stand around all nervous-like, not sure if they should sit down or run for the hills.

"I. Said. Sit," she repeats, teeth clenched, spitting each word out like a dragon breathing fireballs.

I cross my arms and look away from her. It's a total pissy baby move, I know, but it's really good for driving grownups insane. "No," I say and stare at a random spot on the ceiling.

"Sit!" she yells, louder this time. Out of the corner of my eye, I see a few of the other kids jump a little bit. They watch the show. Someone peels off from the group and heads into the hallway. Maybe he's off to get some popcorn and soda. Or maybe to alert the authorities.

Is she really that stupid? She thinks she knows me just because of some other teacher's hateful gossip, but she has no freakin' clue. She thinks she can yell at me and make me bend like one of those floppy car dealership noodle dudes.

But she's so, so wrong.

Behind what she thinks she knows about me is a rock-hard wall. You don't live how I live and survive without one. I've been screamed at my whole life: by Dad, by Mom, by my aunts and uncles, by my grandparents, by the people on my street, by my teachers, by random assholes on the sidewalk, by the cops chasing me away from the "respectable" parts of town. I used to flinch and hide and cry, but all it does now is piss me off.

And when I get pissed off, I yell. Just like they do. And let me tell you, I can yell and scream and curse with the best of them. What's a kid like me supposed to do? It's not like I can slap that tight-lipped little smirk off of her face like Ugly Me really wants to.

I may be screwed up, but I'm not an idiot.

My tongue has been honed to a razor-sharp point by all the

bullshit I've put up with, and I'm ready to unleash it.

"I'm not asking again! Sit down right now!" she yells again.

I take a deep breath...

Chapter 6

BUT BEFORE I can open my mouth to spew hot words, I feel a gentle tap on the back of my arm. I snatch my arm away and spin to face this new threat, tense and coiled, a bony, half-starved seventh-grade snake ready to strike.

"Randi," says a gentle, familiar voice. No yelling, no threatening, none of that other power trip "because I'm a grownup and you're just some crummy kid" crap. One soft word broke through the rising red tide of fight, fight, fight. I feel my overheated jets cooling down fast. I wouldn't be surprised if the room filled with steam right about now.

"Mr. B?" I say, surprised to see him here and glad that he came in when he did and didn't have to witness Ugly Me opening a can of seventh-grade crazy on this lady. Mr. Breckenridge was my sixth-grade math teacher and one of the few human beings I could stand last year.

"Can you come talk to me, please?" he asks before turning around and walking away. And before I realize what's happening, and before Ugly Me can buck up again and screw everything up, my soggy, milk-soaked feet follow his gentle words through the parting crowd and out the door. Something about the way he asks instead of commanding, yelling, giving that looking down "I smell something that stinks" frowny-face that makes me feel like a bug--something I don't really understand but can feel in my whole body--makes me want to follow.

I feel like an old, deflated birthday balloon as I follow him out the door. Out of the corner of my eye, I catch glimpses of a variety of faces: some concerned, some nervous, some amused. Those smirks cut deep.

I've just put on a show. Not a fun, bingeable Netflix cupcake show, but one of those old, nasty circus sideshows.

And I'm the screwed-up, too-stupid, too-skinny freak with an anger problem that no one wants to notice but can't quite look away from.

Math lady slams the door behind us so hard that the weird little door window rattles like it's going to break. I sort of wish the thing would shatter into a million pieces and shred my face off. But I'm not that lucky. I press my forehead against the cold metal of the lockers. They smell like fresh paint, and I pray that I don't come away from this with a bright green splotch on my head.

"Randi," says Mr. B., "do you remember what I told you back in May? Just before you left for the summer?"

I don't say anything. The metal feels good against my face, like when I flip my sweaty pillow when the nightmares come. As my anger cools, hot tears begin to slide down my cheeks.

"You have such beauty inside, just waiting to shine," he continues, not waiting for me to answer, knowing that I know because he told me a hundred times. "But you have to let it out, Randi. You can't control the crap that gets dealt to you, but you've got to control how you respond to it."

My words return, and I wipe salty tears with the back of my hand and sniff. It's ugly and snotty and loud. "I know, Mr. B., but it's so hard. You don't know what I've--"

"You're right, Randi, I don't know what it's like to be you. You've told me a few things, but I know I don't know the half of it." He lets off this deep sigh and puts on a warm half-smile. "I'm glad to see you. Not so much like this already, but I'm glad you're here."

I turn around and slide down the wall. The weird little vent things in the lockers scrape against my bony back. I pull my legs into my chest and hug them tight. I take a few deep breaths. I swear my shoes are already starting to smell even worse than they did before. Putrid milk mixed in with a year's worth of sweat and dirt.

"I don't know what's wrong with me." I do another gross, snotty sniff, "I just get so mad so easy--"

"Listen," Mr. B. interrupts. "I get pissed off, too, when I hear people talking to each other the way she was talking to you."

"Really?" I'm kind of caught off-guard by his very non-teacher-y use of "pissed." I mean, I know that teachers are regular people, too (supposedly), but it's still weird to hear it from him.

"But I also don't like to see you like that, either."

"Yeah, but she--"

"It doesn't matter," he says. "There's always going to be someone or something there to step in and try to dim your sunshine, whether it's the first day of seventh grade or some random Thursday at the grocery store."

Mr. Gorley walks by and stops in front of me. He's wearing these shiny brown leather shoes with bright purple laces that look like they came from clown shoes. Looks like someone's been reading some men's fashion blogs this summer.

"Hi Miranda," he says. I keep my face buried in my knees and don't reply, but he doesn't seem to want to press the issue. He's been around enough kids like me to know when to back off. I look up to catch Mr. B. giving him an "I got this" type of look. Mr. Gorley nods and takes his weird shoelaces on down the hallway.

"Anyway," says Mr. B. "It's not what makes you mad or how often you get mad that defines you. It's all about how you act when you're mad."

"That's easy for you to say. I've never seen you get mad." I look up at him. I just now notice that he's wearing his hair pulled back into a little bun on the back of his head. A thick gray headband keeps everything else tidy. Geez. What a dork.

"Come on, now," he says. "I teach math to a bunch of sixth-grade lunatics for a living. Don't think for a minute that I don't want to go into an ugly rage, like, twenty times a day." He grins at me and reaches down his hand. There's a tan line where a ring used to be. "So if I can refrain from inflicting bodily harm on a bunch of sixth graders, then you can make it through Ms. Odum's math class."

I take his hand and allow him to lift me into a standing position. I return his smile and wipe my eyes one last time. He's right. If I were him, I would've killed me last year after all the crap I pulled. Seriously.

As I turn the doorknob to face math class again, I turn to Mr. B. "You missed the boat on the man bun, like, two years ago."

He smiles. "There she is," he says.

I take a deep breath and walk back into the classroom.

Chapter 7

THE FLOORS IN the gym are all new and shiny. And the fumes from the new paint or varnish or whatever they used are strong. After two minutes in the gym, I'm feeling lightheaded. Much more of this and I'll be floating.

The whistle jockeys in here must already be high. Why else would they want to make a bunch of middle schoolers run on the first day of school? All around me, kids complain and shuffle their feet as they run around the gym. Correction: after an entire summer of video game binges and marathon napping and minimal physical activity, I wouldn't exactly call what they're doing "running."

One guy takes maybe two laps and runs into the locker room, his hand over his mouth, holding back the flood of half-digested Cap'n Crunch. A few drops splatter on the floor before he makes it through the door, and I hear him ralphing inside. A high-pitched squeal echoes through the gym, and the lady gym teacher runs to assist, her slick red pants swish-swishing all the way. I guess he didn't see the "Girls'" sign on the door.

I feel a little better about my milky shoes.

A girl from my science class is clutching her stomach and talking to Mr. Shaw, one of the guy gym teachers. She has tears in her eyes and is spilling some story about periods and cramps. Nice move. That kind of talk is like poison to the male population around here. He looks uncomfortable and tells her to just have a seat. Must be the most convenient cramps ever. Just before gym, I saw her chasing a cute blonde kid through the hallway.

I actually don't mind the running. I spent most of my summer walking around the city to avoid my mom and her angry outbursts, incoherent crazy talk, and constant string of random strange visitors. I'll bet I walked, like, a thousand miles this summer.

Walking around like that is totally peaceful in some weird kind of way. And as I walk around, I get to watch all sorts of people. Like the lady who lives down my street and takes her baby out in his stroller at noon each day. She looks dirt poor like me and Mom and always wears this ratty yellow dress. But the way she coos and sings and talks to that cute little chunker of a baby of hers, you'd think she was the richest lady in town. They just float right along in this crappy, beat-up stroller, smiling and laughing and living all fairy tale happy.

I wonder what that feels like.

And there's this dude I see a lot when I walk around downtown. He's this old guy who dresses in an old brown suit and hat. Kind of like something you'd see in an old movie or something. His white hair is all crazy, and he babbles on and on to anyone who will stop and listen. You can't understand a word he says, but he's totally serious about whatever he's saying. He just scoots around all day, trying to find someone who will listen to him. And when someone is nice enough, or maybe gullible enough, to stop and listen, the guy just beams.

I think he's my spirit animal.

When I walk, I get to escape my life. I become a tourist in the lives of others. But not in a creepy stalker way. More like window shopping like people do in old movies.

As I run, my feet squeak--eek, eek, eek--on the sticky gym floor. I run fast and hard and easy, and the day's crap begins to flush itself away as I breathe deep and pound the floorboards: the cafeteria, the stupid girls in science class, the yelling in math class. After a whole summer of hitting the pavement in the heat and sort-of sleeping in a hot and sweaty mess, it feels great to run in the air-conditioned gym, even with the floor fumes singeing my nose hairs.

Eek, eek, eek, eek--my body moves and my mind rests, and while everyone around me is wheezing and panting like a bunch of pugs, I feel like I could run forever. But then real-life slaps me in the freaking face once again and reminds me that I'm an idiot for thinking that there's something good for me here.

Or, more accurately, the gym floor slaps me in the face.

Chapter 8

I LIE THERE, hurting and embarrassed all over again. It gets
super quiet in the gym while everyone wrestles with whether to
laugh or be concerned and rush to my aid. It's like a full-on war
zone in here; I can almost hear the internal conflicts raging.

I guess I did pay attention in English class at least once last
year.

I use that precious few seconds to lie there all alone and try to
figure out what the hell happened. I sit up and take an inventory.
I appear to be all in one piece, and all of my bodily fluids seem
to be sloshing around inside me where they belong. I feel a
strange draft and look down at my foot, hoping that I don't see a
blood-soaked stump.

What I see is much worse.

My shoe is completely wrecked. The sole is almost completely
torn off and just kind of flops there, holding on for dear life by
the heel. Maybe milk does some weird chemical-y thing to the
fibers in shoes, or maybe the sticky new floor must have been too
much for my shoe to handle. Or it could have something to do
with the fact that I've been wearing these same cheap-o hand-me-
downs pretty much 24-7 for two years.

Mr. Shaw runs over and kneels down. His legs are super hairy-
-like total Sasquatch mode. "Are you okay?" he asks. "That was
quite a spill."

"Yeah, I'm alright," I say, "but my shoe." I nod toward my
busted sneaker.

"Oh geez," he says. He reaches down and pinches my shoe

back together with big, meaty hands. His knuckles are super hairy, too. I just now notice that my toes are poking out through a hole in my ratty sock. "Do you have another pair at home that you could wear?"

Now it's time for my own internal conflict. Shots fire inside my mind as I try to decide what to tell him. Do I tell him the truth? That these stinky messes are the only shoes I've had in two years, given to me as too-large, already-worn hand-me-downs by some random distant relative I've never met? Supposedly. Should I tell him that I think my mom actually stole these shoes from a neighbor's front porch and gave them to me so she wouldn't have to spend the cash on them?

Or do I try to pretend that I'm some version of a normal kid whose parents do normal parent things like buy their kids shoes and kiss them goodbye and tuck them into actual beds all safe and warm at night? Do I lie and fake that I'm not a broke nothing?

If I lie, I'll have to come up with an excuse each day about why I didn't bring gym shoes. He'll get sick of the excuses and obvious lies and probably get sick of me and I'll fail gym like a total loser.

But if I tell the truth, he'll probably feel sorry for me and offer to buy me some new shoes. He seems like that kind of guy. One of those weirdos who actually likes kids like me for some reason. I don't understand people like him. He seems like a smart, well-adjusted, somewhat normal human being. He could be doing pretty much anything right now, but he chooses to spend his days herding feral middle schoolers. We're like a bunch of tweaked-out kittens with acne.

For a second, I'm tempted to actually tell the truth and fess up to being a penniless joke. But that feeling is chased away by Ugly Me with claws out.

You don't need his pity!

But I do need a new pair of shoes.

You'll figure it out! You've done everything else on your own for years!

But it actually kind of feels good for someone to--

But then he'll always look at you like that poor, pitiful kid that he bought those shoes for! You'll never live it down!

Is that such a bad thing?

What will Mom say if she sees us come in with new shoes? Remember what happened when Ms. Tuttle gave you that jacket?

I look up at Mr. Shaw. "Um, yeah, I'm...I'm good."

Because I do remember the jacket. I remember her face, a furious, totally un-motherlike messed-up combo of shame and jealousy. She punished me for having what she couldn't give me. Took it out on me.

Ms. Tuttle noticed that I never wore the jacket again, so I lied and told her that I had lost it.

I start thinking of new lies to tell Mr. Shaw when I don't show up with gym shoes. Since it's only the first day, I'm going to need a lot of them.

Chapter 9

AFTER GYM, I head down to the school's basement for Practical Arts. It's this class where some psycho with a teaching license gives a bunch of middle schoolers power tools and knives and hot glue guns and expects us to make things without maiming each other or committing manslaughter. (Childslaughter?) I don't know whose idea this was, but I can't decide if I'm excited or terrified out of my little seventh-grade mind.

Who am I kidding? I've always liked making things, and the thought that, at any moment, I could witness a horrific accidental dismemberment gives me some sort of creepy thrill. I don't know why that is, but I don't like to dwell in that part of my mind for very long.

Ms. Alvarez is our licensed nutcase. She's this super-pretty lady with gorgeous black hair pulled back in a tight, no-nonsense bun. I think she'd look better with her hair down, but I guess she probably wears it that way so she doesn't catch her hair in one of these scary-looking machines down here and get her scalp ripped off like some horrible wet hairy hat.

Our classroom has no windows, and it totally reeks with all of these post-gym sweaty preteens crammed into it. Seriously. It smells like a swamp's butthole down here. I try to give my armpit a sneaky sniff just to make sure I'm not a major contributor to the funk, but this cute blonde guy catches me mid-whiff. He smirks and looks away. My face turns red, and I totally try to play it cool by transitioning into a big, fake yawn. I don't think he buys it.

I don't know why I even care. It's not like any sane male member of this species would be interested in an ugly, uninteresting me.

I sit down at this old-school wood table with, like, a thousand years' worth of graffiti carved into it. I don't feel like talking to anyone, so I stare at the table and read: "Jimmy wuz here," "Mr. Stone is a jabroni," "Katie is a hore," "Beavis and Butthead rules," "Alisha is a bit--"

"Can I sit here?" asks a too-happy voice. I look up. It's this perky blonde with a wide, pink cheerleader hair bow and a mouthful of serious hardware smiling down at me. I guess she's new or something because I don't recognize her from last year. Then again, last year I missed a ton of school and barely talked to anyone when I actually showed up. And when I was here, I spent the majority of my time locked up in in-school suspension because I guess my teachers didn't want to bother with me.

"Uh...I guess so," I say. Wow, Randi. Go easy on the enthusiasm. You'd hate to scare her away by coming on too strong before she has a chance to get to know you and then run away screaming.

"Thanks!" she says and flashes another metallic grin as she plops down in the seat across from me. She reaches out a hand with what has to be the best nail job I've ever seen. Each nail except the ring finger is painted with a tiny beach scene complete with sand, water, and an umbrella (each finger sporting a different-colored one). On her ring finger is a bright yellow sun in dark sunglasses beaming a friendly smile. "Name's Emmaline. Emmaline Wilson."

I reach out and shake her hand. "I'm Miranda Lewis," I say, "but most people call me Randi." Well, the people who bother to call me anything do, anyway. I stare at my hand in hers for a little too long and we cross into the awkward, okay-now-we're-technically-holding-hands territory. My hand seems so plain and dirty inside this bright and perfectly-manicured specimen. Ugly Me takes over, and I snatch my hand away as if her hand was a red-hot snake with leprosy or something. I look back down at the table. I feel much more at home among the scars, chipped paint, and profanity.

"Nice to meet you," she says, still sporting that big smile. She leans back and puts this ginormous granny-style purse on the table. It lands with a thud, and the whole table shakes like it's going to shatter into splinters. It's printed with unicorns and rainbows and must weigh, like, a million pounds or something.

"Nice purse," I say, my voice dripping sarcasm, Ugly Me getting ready to have a field day with this too-happy weirdo.

"Thanks! I made it myself!" I don't know if she missed the bitchiness in my voice or if she just decided to ignore it and press on with her freaky positivity. Either way, I'm caught off-guard, and Ugly Me slinks back into the shadows a little bit.

But just a little. Because Ugly Me is always there, just beneath the surface, ready to pounce out and eat someone's face off.

"Yeah...um...that's actually pretty cool," I say. And this time, there's no snippy, hate-drenched sarcasm because I actually do think that it's pretty cool that she made the thing. I mean, I'm not into unicorns or that kind of cutesy stuff, but I'm kind of impressed. I wonder if she makes one in a thunderstorm gray? That would jive with my motif a little better. Plus, I'm deadly curious about what the heck she keeps in that thing.

She doesn't skip a beat. "Thanks, Randi! I make stuff all the time. It's, like, literally all I do when I'm not in school. I want to open an online store, but my dad says I'm too young for it. Here, check this out!" She reaches into the bag, and I half-expect it to swallow her whole like some kind of evil purse monster from one of those cheesy old horror movies or something. She pulls out a tiny little something and puts it into my hand.

It's this clear-ish plastic-y ring. It looks like something you'd get out of those red quarter junk machines like they put at the entrances to grocery stores. I'm not impressed, and it must show because she nudges me.

"Hold it up to the light and look closer!" Ugly Me yearns to break out and squash her annoying enthusiasm, but I shove her back into the dark.

I hold the ring up to the light, and what I see makes my jaw drop.

Chapter 10

I COULDN'T TELL from just holding it in my hand, but the thing is filled with what must be thousands of teeny-tiny air bubbles. And as I stare at it, all stupid-looking and open-mouthed, I move it around in front of my eyes. The light dances off of those tiny specks and creates what looks like a million little stars. It looks like one of those pictures you see on computer wallpapers where the sky looks like it goes on forever with little points of light. It's amazing.

I've never seen one of those beautiful starry skies in person. I've only ever seen the sky above this place. At night, the city lights bleed over and give it this sick, washed-out look. Instead of a gorgeous, black, star-spotted blanket, we get a sky that looks like it's about to gag because it has to hang over this shithole.

One of these days, I'm going get out of this miserable place and move to a place where the sky goes on forever. And there I'll have a yard that's more than a tiny patch of grass covered in seven layers of dog crap and garbage. I'm going to lie there every night and just stare up at the sky and follow those little points of starshine until I lose myself in them.

And when I have kids, they're going to have a place right beside me and we can get lost together. And there we will be, away from all this: the yelling, the bullying, the fighting, the anger, the drugs, the drama, the ugliness. And we will all be safe and warm with lots of love to go around.

I get totally lost inside this little plastic ring, staring into those starry points of light. I feel tears forming big wet lumps in my eyes, threatening to spill out and betray me. I shake my head like I just took a serious blow to the old cranium and come to my senses.

I'm not staring into an endless starry sky. I'm contemplating the meaning of my meaningless existence because of a crappy hunk of discount store junk. I feel like a total space cadet for it, and the sting of real life comes crashing down on me.

Because here's the bullshit reality of the situation: I'll be lucky to make it out of high school in one piece. And if I do, it'll take a miracle for me to take my miserable self any farther than my own block. I'm stuck up to my ears in my muddy life, and unless someone comes along soon and pulls me out (they probably won't), I'm going to drown in the smelly muck of it all.

Stupid stars. Stupid me for letting myself believe that I could have a piece of life beyond my here and now.

I hand the ring back to Emmaline. I catch her looking at me with that "What the hell is going on here?" kind of face. Ugly Me wants to rip her lips off for it. I feel like a helpless, flipped-over bug, and I wait for her hurtful words to smash me to a gooey pulp.

But that hurt doesn't come.

"Why don't you keep it?" she asks and hands the ring back to me. "I think maybe you need it more than I do."

I don't know what to say. What's her play, here? I shake my head and offer it back to her.

"No. Seriously. You take it." She grabs my hand and closes my fingers around the ring. She leans in to me and her voice gets all whisper-serious. "I think it...chose you or something. Like in *The Lord of the Rings*."

Oh, Jesus. What a nerd. Of course, I get the reference, so what does that say about me? A smile sneaks its way onto my lips. *Be careful, Randi*, a voice inside me warns.

I slip the ring onto my finger. It fits perfectly.

"Thank you," I say.

She smiles back.

Chapter 11

I WAIT FOR the bell to ring to dismiss us to lunch. I'm super hungry after Ugly Me threw a big hissy fit and dumped my breakfast this morning. So stupid. I haven't eaten anything since yesterday's lunchtime ramen.

Ms. Alvarez has just enough time to scare the crap out of all of us by telling us all about the million and one ways we can kill or disfigure ourselves on the equipment in her room. I can't tell if she's really seen some stuff go down down here or if she's got the craziest imagination ever. Either way, I think she set the world record for the longest "Randi listening quietly to a teacher without going bananas" session.

She tells us this one story that she calls "The Picture Day Disaster." She gets really dramatic quiet when she tells it. We all lean in to hear.

"It was back in '97, and it was my first year as a teacher. That was back when this was just wood shop, like in all those schools in TV sitcoms. Think of kids with saws and hammers, making birdhouses. Splinters everywhere, sawdust floating in the air. That was pretty much it. No computers, no 3D printers, nothing." She gestures around all dramatically as if she's some model on a game show. I have to admit it. There's a lot of pretty cool stuff down here.

"It was picture day. It was a big deal back then. Before selfies. Before everything had a built-in camera. Kids even used to dress up for it." She stares off into the distance and looks a little bit lost for a second. She gives a big sigh and continues.

"Cooper Davidson dressed up. He wore this adorable shirt and tie. I can still see it to this day. It was a white shirt with a blue tie. Little yellow ducks all over it. The tie, that is." She stops and sighs again. "He was running the drill press that day, making a new climbing peg board for the gym class. I told him to tuck that tie into his shirt, but he didn't listen..." Her voice trails off and she gets really quiet.

"He was drilling right along, almost finished, but then before we knew it, that cute little tie got wrapped up in the drill and pulled him right in." Ms. Alvarez starts breathing hard and talking faster. "We couldn't stop it. All we could see was the blood, and we panicked. It was everywhere: on the walls, on the floor, on the ceiling. He was screaming and we were screaming and we just watched in horror." Tears are coming to her eyes now and she's starting to sound hysterical. "By the time Janet Mitton thought to unplug the machine, poor Cooper's face had been completely ripped off and splattered around the room. It took weeks to clean up the bloodstains. In fact, if you look up there," she gestures toward a spot on the ceiling, "you can see where they missed a spot."

Our eyes follow her finger as she points. I've never heard a middle school classroom this quiet before. We stare at the ceiling, hoping-but-not-hoping to see a decades-old bloodstain. The silence deepens.

"BOOGA BOOGA BOOGA!" Ms. Alvarez shouts. The entire class jumps like ten feet into the air. I swear to God I pee a little in my pants.

She laughs a big, goofy laugh for a good minute or so, tears rolling down her cheeks. "I love doing that!" she says. "I wait all summer long to tell that story! I think you guys set a new height record!" She's still laughing, and those of us whose hearts have started beating again are starting to join in. Emmaline looks like she's about to puke.

"Come on, guys," Ms. Alvarez says. "How old do you think I am? I was 14 years old in '97, for crying out loud!" She puts her hands on her hips and pretends to act all offended that we would believe that she was old enough to have been a teacher that long ago.

"But seriously," she says, and her voice hardens a bit. "Listen to what I say because I don't want to see any of you get hurt because you're my babies now, and I love you." She looks around and smiles, and I believe her.

I wonder if she'd adopt a mess like me.

Chapter 12

BY THE TIME I get to the lunchroom, some idiot has already burned a bag of popcorn in the beat-up communal microwave. The whole place smells like someone took a pair of sweaty gym socks, soaked them in garbage water for a month, and set them on fire. People are making a huge freaking show of holding their noses and pretending to gag. One stupid girl stuffs her head into the trash can and retches loudly. The dramatics are more sickening to me than the actual smell.

The guilty party is nowhere to be seen. With all the immature bull going on in here, they're probably too embarrassed to admit to the deed. I can't say I blame them. The microwave just drones on until smoke starts to seep through the cracks of the door. Finally, Mr. Gorley runs over and turns the thing off. He opens the door, and a huge cloud of smoke puffs out as the bag bursts into flames.

He panics and snatches a chocolate milk off of some chubby kid's tray. He douses the flames and pours the milk all down his pants in the process. It puts the fire out, but the smell goes from simply horrible to crisis-level, Taco Bell bathroom-like bio-hazard. A couple of kids throw up for real this time. The poor microwave looks like a war zone.

Mr. Gorley shakes his head and looks around the cafeteria, hoping that someone will do the right thing and take responsibility for the horrendous, stanky mess. Or at least just offer to help. He deflates like last week's birthday balloons. He looks a bit defeated, and I can't help but feel sorry for him. I'm sure he didn't spend all those years in college just so he could deal with crap like this.

Middle schoolers can be like vicious wild dogs. With razor-sharp teeth. And BO. And wicked acne. You can't forget the zits.

I sneak past the pitiful scene and slide into the serving line. School sustenance, take two. I just hope some of the food manages to make it to my mouth this time. Today's lunch is dinosaur-shaped chicken chunks, limp broccoli, and neon-yellow macaroni and cheese that I swear to God I saw a lunch lady pour out of a giant plastic bag. I wonder for a second what ungodly things they must do to the poor chicken at the factory to somehow stamp a happy little brontosaurus out of its carcass, but I decide to think of something happier. Like root canals or rainstorms.

I make it to the front of the line without spazzing out and causing another disaster. So far, so good. The same lunch lady from this morning, the new one, recognizes me and gives me this "you poor thing" smile and waves me through. I guess she now knows what a pitiful excuse for a human I am. Word travels fast.

I stand off to the side for a second and watch the other kids shuffle through the line and hand over crisp checks written by mommy and daddy and buy ice creams and Cheetos and those weird super sweet juice-but-not-juice drinks they sell as "healthy" alternatives to sodas.

One day, I'd like to know what it feels like to be completely taken care of like these kids. To have parents who know where I am all the time. To have a mom who waits outside the school for me and embarrasses me by telling me she missed me and asks me how my day was. To have a dad who isn't locked up for God knows how long.

Instead, I orbit around my mom like a scrawny, twitchy moon. I want to be pulled in by her gravity, but every time I get too close, some horrible natural disaster occurs. Lots of screaming and crying and hurt.

There are a bunch of pictures of Baby Me in this old shoebox at home. I pull them out sometimes and look at them. I recognize the faces of the people in the photos, but looking at them is like taking a glimpse into some sort of wacky alternate reality where people smile and hug and laugh.

There's this one picture of me and Dad that I used to look at a lot. I'm probably two or three and dressed in this little Mickey Mouse shirt that comes down to my knees. He and I have our faces scrunched together, and my little cheek is all mushed up against his. We're both smiling into the camera. In the picture, he has this stubbly beard.

I swear I can still feel it against my face sometimes.

He used to grab me up when he came home from work and rub his face against mine. His whiskers would tickle me. I would laugh and laugh and say, "Stop it, Daddy!" even though I didn't really want him to stop. He would laugh and laugh and keep tickling me until we both were so tickled we couldn't breathe because the happy was taking all the breath away.

This was way before things all went to shit and Ugly Me came around.

When the Bad started to happen, I would sometimes take out that picture and whisper little prayers for things to go back the way they were. I would rock back and forth and squeeze my eyes closed and wish myself back into that picture.

Clearly, it didn't work. That happy little girl and her happy little daddy are dead--swallowed up by ugliness. I might as well sell that photo to some picture frame company to use as the cheesy filler photos. We'll fit right in with the pictures of the other fictional families.

"Out of the way, freak!" yells a voice behind me. Present reality comes rushing back to me, and the shoebox fades away. I've been spaced out again. I look back. It's one of the girls from science class, one of the ones that received my one-finger salute.

"What are you looking at, Dumpster Girl?" she asks, curling her stupid lip up with this disgusted-looking face like she just stepped on a fresh dog turd. She's slathered head-to-toe in mall clothes and makeup. She's got this glittery pink headband in her perfect blonde hair that Ugly Me would just love to rip off and shove sideways up her preppy you-know-what.

I stare her down, and she puffs up a little bit. "I said," she takes a step closer, "what are you loo--"

"Girl, you'd better take your little self outta my kitchen right now!" says another voice. It's Miss Ruthie, and she's evidently seen the whole little shebang because she's got her flabby arms crossed and looks super pissed.

The girl opens her mouth to argue but thinks better of it when Miss Ruthie cocks her head and give her a wicked stinkeye. She looks down and squeezes past me. Miss Ruthie rubs her hands together like she's cleaning them and gives me a big grin.

"I got you, girlie," she says.

I walk back into the cafeteria with a smile on my face.

Chapter 13

I'M ABLE TO ride the wave of pleasant feelings left behind from Miss Ruthie's kindness for a whopping 30 seconds before crash landing right back into Headband Girl and her cronies. That's probably a new world record for Randi Lewis Good Vibes. It was nice while it lasted.

They're all huddled together at a table in a corner, and they're chitchatting at about a thousand miles an hour. I try to tell myself that they could be talking about any stupid old thing, but they're all staring hate right at me. I know they're talking about me, and the words that I can't even hear cut me deep and wash away the good (what little there was), leaving only Ugly Me left behind. Their over-makeuped eyes follow me as I struggle (and fail) to ignore them while simultaneously struggling (and failing) to find a seat next to a familiar face who won't immediately pepper spray me or run away screaming.

My heart starts to beat fast as my seat search starts to get a little bit desperate. I want to blend in with the crowd and hide from the disgusted faces and the soundless hatewords. I can't help but to keep looking over at them, and each time I do, I feel like I'm being punched in the spleen or something. I start to breathe hard as panic floods me.

When I was six, I was riding in the car with Mom. That was way back when we actually had a working car and didn't have to hoof it or bum rides all the time. We were going home from the store, and I was crying. I don't remember what for. Probably whining about something stupid.

Mom was in one of her moods and kept telling me to shut up. I guess I just kept crying and crying because the next thing I knew, she was slamming on the brakes and screaming at me to get out of the car. She screamed so loud I almost peed my pants, so I hopped out like she asked me to.

She drove off and left me.

We weren't that far from home, but I was young and sad and scared. So scared. I looked around, but nothing seemed familiar to me. I started walking, following Mom's taillights down the street, but she turned and drove out of sight.

I took the street that I thought my mom did, but it was the wrong one. My little feet walked and walked and walked. I passed a million little houses that looked nothing like mine. I cried and cried and cried.

I do remember why I cried that cry.

It was getting dark, and I couldn't find my house. The more I walked, the scareder I became and the harder it was to breathe. A thousand cars passed by, but no one stopped to help a lost little girl.

By the time I found my house, I was shivering despite the fact that it was 80 degrees outside. When I walked in, Mom yelled at me and asked me where the hell I'd been. She sent me to my room without dinner that night.

That was before I got used to it.

I feel a tap on my shoulder, and I flinch. I spin around and Ugly Me faces a smallish chubby kid that I don't recognize. He's wearing a worn-out Minecraft shirt, and he's got a serious homemade bowl cut. "Don't touch me, asshole!" I shout, and the kid turns a bright shade of pink and looks like he's about to cry. He tries to say something, but the words get stuck. He just turns around and sits back down.

He's sitting at a table by himself. He's got his back to me, but I can hear him sniffling. Ugly Me shrinks just a little bit.

I walk over and sit down across from him.

Chapter 14

HE'S RUBBING TEARS from his eyes. He tries to hide it by staring down at his tray as if he's reading his fortune in the curves of his dinosaur nuggets. Ugly Me made those tears without even thinking, but, for some crazy reason, I want to fix it.

Ugly Me protests. *You don't even know this kid. Why do you even care how he feels?* And I have to admit: a big part of me wants to not care and just sit there across from this mystery nobody and eat my lunch in peace. But I look up and can still see the faces of Headband Girl and the others, still staring, still talking.

I hurt, but that doesn't mean that I get to make other people hurt. That was something Mr. B told me all the time last year. Ugly Me retreats for now. But she doesn't go far. Just hides in the shadows, waiting for a chance to slither out again.

She never has to wait very long.

"Hey," I say to the top of the kid's bent-over head. In addition to the worst bowlcut of all time, this kid is sporting a gnarly homemade color job. I'm guessing Kool-Aid. His scalp is dyed a bright pink and his reddish-brown hair looks like he's suffered a very recent bleeding head wound. Poor kid. "Sorry about that. That was super bitchy of me." He wipes his eyes again and raises his head a little bit.

"I-I just wanted to--"

"I know. You were trying to be nice, but I totally crapped in your face." I sigh. I feel like a huge jerk. This poor kid didn't deserve this.

He starts to smile. "Ew," he says.

I roll my eyes. Do boys ever grow out of this stupid bathroom humor phase? "Anyway, I really am sorry."

"S'okay," he says. He looks at me. His eyes are totally red and swollen. He's a super ugly crier. Wow. This kid's got everything going for him. He must be my long-lost brother or something.

"My name's Randi. Short for Miranda. Lewis," I say. "What's yours?"

He hesitates. "Achilles Johnson," he says, his voice flat as week-old roadkill. I try to stifle the laugh that begs to blast out of my mouth. I fail, and it comes out as a loud snort. Like, total Old MacDonald E-I-E-I-O piggy stuff. He shows me the top of his pink scalp again.

"Wow," I say, trying hard-but-not-hard-enough to not laugh in his face. I'm still giggling when I add, "Sorry, it's just you look more like a...well...*not* an Achilles."

He looks back up at me. He sighs. "I'm used to it. Not many kids named 'Achilles' runnin' around these days."

"Yeah. Well, your parents must have been on some real strong stuff to come up with that. What were they thinking?"

"Hard to say," he says. "If I had to guess, probably something like, 'Yay. Another damn baby. Let's go do a bunch of drugs now.'"

"Oh," I say. I mean, what do I say to that? Wow. Awkward. But totally familiar in a sad sort of way.

He waves his hand around like he's swatting invisible flies. "Anyway, I picked that name when I got adopted. When they brought me home, they let me pick any name I wanted."

"So...were *you* high, then?"

He laughs. "No, but I was eight, and I was in the middle of this big Greek mythology phase. I'd been reading those *Percy Jackson* books. So I named myself after my favorite Greek hero."

"*O*-kay then," I say. "Did they not have, like, veto powers or something?" I try to think of what name my eight-year-old self would've chosen. Probably Rainbow Unicorn or Princess Glam-Glam or Glitter Moonbeam Sparkle or something like that.

"Nope. Just turned me loose and let me go at it. I sometimes think that they adopted me as part of some weird experiment. Like, they're just observing me like some lab rat and they're just waiting for me to totally screw my life up so they can write some book about me and make a million bucks."

"So...what's your middle name?" I ask.

"You have to promise not to make fun of me," he says.

"Sure," I reply. What could be worse than Achilles, anyway?

He looks around all sideways to make sure the coast is clear. I take a sip of the not-very-cold milk on my tray. "Skywalker," he says.

My nostrils erupt into flame as jets of milk shoot out of them and onto my chicken nuggets. The laughter comes so hard that there's no stopping it. "Are...you...freaking...serious?" I ask, the words interrupted by milky giggles.

"You said you wouldn't make fun of me!"

"Yeah, but that was before you told me your middle name was 'Skywalker!' *Je-sus!* You seriously expect me to just act like that's normal or whatever?"

"Give me a break! I told you I was only eight years old."

"Sorry," I say, "Just...just...wow."

"Yeah. 'Wow' is right." He starts to laugh. I start to feel an honest-to-goodness smile spread across my face.

"Thanks for letting me sit with you," I say.

"You're welcome," he says. "You looked like you were about to lose it. What was up with that?"

I nod toward Headband Girl. "See that girl over there with the pink headband?"

He turns around and scans the cafeteria. "The one with all the makeup?"

"Yeah. That's her."

"Well, what about her?" he asks.

I tell him about science class and the whole "Dumpster Girl" comment and the gab session with her goons. "She's just being a total ass to me. I don't know what her problem is."

"So why do you care? I mean, you don't even know her name. So what if she's talking crap about you?"

Oh. He's one of those. Every now and then I'll run into one of these "Screw 'em! Who cares what they think?" freakazoids. I have no clue how they do it. I wish my brain worked that way. I'd love to just forget all the nasty looks, harsh tones, yelling, whispered words, and painful jabs that are thrown my way from so many people. I want to be a cool little cucumber and just deal, but I have no freaking clue how to do it.

No matter how hard I try to be strong and just let things bounce off of me like all that "I'm rubber and you're glue" first-grade bullshit, the hurt keeps piling up like a tower of cards just waiting to crash down and slice me to ribbons with a million stinging paper cuts.

Sticks and stones? That's the biggest lie they've ever told. People say that because they're too lazy or too exhausted or too apathetic to listen. I've been kicked, slapped, choked, punched, and everything else you can think of. But none of that crap hurts as much as those little invisible words cutting into me like dull, rusty knives.

These thoughts bring Ugly Me slinking out of the darkness. I feel the burning wet creeping across my eyes.

The bell rings, and I bail without giving him an answer.

Chapter 15

THE READING TEACHER, this lady with trendy round glasses, bright red lipstick, and bleached-out hair with arrow-straight bangs tries to get us to wake up by having us write about what we did on summer vacation. I think this is her first year teaching because she looks like she could be somebody's older high school sister. Plus, she doesn't have that flattened, perpetually worn-out look like a lot of the older teachers do.

I have to bum a piece of paper and a pencil from a kid sitting next to me. He's got this backpack loaded down with so many notebooks and pencils and crap that he looks like he's hoarding for some school supply apocalypse. I don't even know how he walks with that thing on his back. He'll be crippled by Christmas if he keeps this up.

Not that this is anything to be proud of, but I've become quite the little scavenger. I've learned how to work a room and scrape together what I need. The key is to not ask the same person too many times in the same week. And you'd be shocked at how many pencils and pens can be found on the floors of a middle school. It's kind of sad, really. I try not to think about all the folks working crappy jobs in pencil factories all day long. Do they know what ultimately happens to, like, half of their work?

Once you clean the dust and hair off of them, they work just fine. You might have to ignore a few bite marks sometimes, though. And when you reach down to pick one up, you just have to hope and pray that there aren't any boogers or other mystery crud on it.

I used to ask my teachers for stuff, but I was sick of getting those frustrated looks, eye rolls, lectures, and embarrassing trips to the office. I'd rather look like some chronically irresponsible dweeb than admit that I can't keep up with stuff at home because, with so many people coming in and out, things have a way of disappearing there. Plus, I lost count of the number of times we've been evicted and forced to leave a bunch of stuff behind.

Doomsday Prepper gives this heavy sigh (already?) and hands over a couple sheets of paper. What to write? First of all, this assignment is so freaking cliche. I mean, is there some required teacher college course called *Boring Crap to Make Your Kids Do Every Stinking Year 101* or something?

I do the same thing I do every year. I tell big, fat, whopping lies that make me not look like a total loser. According to my school papers, I've been to Disney World four times, I've visited my grandfather in Seattle and gone to the original Starbucks (I think that's where it is, anyway), I've gone on a week-long fishing trip with my uncle, I've been to a ton of MLB games, and I've spent time at a sleep-away camp in upstate New York.

I don't know if anyone ever buys it or not, but at least it's better than admitting to the truth.

This year, I choose to have simply spent my summer lounging at my aunt's pool. My real aunt jetted off to Arizona when I was a baby. I guess she got smart and realized what a mess her life would turn out to be if she stuck around here. Her name's Lacy, but I've never met her. The only time my mom talks to her is when she gets super desperate and gets the guts to call her up and beg her to send money.

In reality, the closest I got to a pool this summer was fishing five bucks out of the creek in my neighborhood. The creek is this smelly, trash-filled little dribble of a thing. I had to dodge, like, a hundred pieces of broken glass, but I managed to get my hands on it. All-in-all, that was a good day. I've still got the cash stashed inside the hole in the kitchen wall.

I turn the paper in and enter stealth mode and somehow manage to fly under the radar for the rest of the day. I guess after repeating all the "welcome to my class now sit down and shut up here are the rules don't piss me off they don't pay me enough to put up with a bunch of heathen monsters if you don't do what I say I'll give you detention and you'd better pass the state tests or I'll lose my job" blah blah blah all morning long, the teachers are as exhausted as I am. We're all already losing that first day of school buzz and are beginning to have some serious summertime lazy hangovers.

By the time the final bell rings, I'm a flat, emotionally-exhausted pancake.

Chapter 16

I DON'T THINK I can stand to ride the bus home today. My nerves are shot, and Ugly Me is out for blood. I don't know what it is. Middle school kids could be nodding off to sleep in class all day long, but the second they get on a school bus in the afternoon, they go absolutely insane. They act like screaming monkeys on crack. If I was a bus driver, I would drive off a cliff on day one. I know there aren't really any cliffs around here, but I would drive until I found one.

It takes me about an hour to walk home from school, but I don't mind one bit. I'm never really in a hurry to actually get home. There's nothing for me there.

As I walk along, my stomach growls like an angry bear. *Feed me!* I think back to lunch and all that Headband Girl crap and feel like kicking myself for letting her get to me like that. She got all in my head and scrambled things up. I was in such a hurry to leave the cafeteria that I totally forgot to go back and squirrel away some leftovers.

I try to remember the last time Mom came home with some groceries. I can't say for sure, but I think I remember seeing some extra ramen yesterday. I think it was the kind in the pink package that's supposed to taste like shrimp or something. It really tastes like butt, but hey, a girl's gotta eat.

My busted shoe flaps against the pavement as I trudge along. I almost trip, like, every five steps and keep getting little rocks and street crud down inside my holey sock. So between the tripping and the constant gravel dumping, the going is super slow this afternoon.

Priority one: find a way to fix my shoe because asking Mom for a new pair is a hilariously bad idea. It really sucks, but it at least gives me something to think about. If my mind wanders too much, I know Ugly Me will want to obsess over Headband Girl and Ms. Odum and the other crap from today.

I turn onto this little dingy alley-like street that runs through Willow Landing, this old, run-down apartment complex. This is the kind of place that most sane people avoid because it has this serious "wrong part of town" vibe. But I'm the poster child for the wrong part of town, so I feel right at home. I walk along all step, step, trip, dump for a while. The sun is angry, even for the second week of August, and I'm pretty sure I'm sweating in places I didn't even know I could sweat.

Is it just me, or do those school board psychopaths make us start school earlier and earlier each year? I'm not sure what they're going for. If you ask me, locking all us crazy people in together during the heat of the summer is just asking for trouble. I can't think of many things more dangerous than a hot and sweaty gang of seventh-grade hormonal headcases.

Maybe we should strike or something.

This street is usually pretty busy, what with the tons of folks like me wandering around these crappy buildings because they have nothing else to do. If I'm still wasting my life walking these streets in ten years, I hope somebody just goes ahead and puts me out of my misery.

I know there's a 99 percent chance I'll end up stuck here, shuffling around all broke and damaged. But there's that other small part of me that hopes for something better. I look down at the ring that Emmaline gave me. I hold my hand up to the sun and look at the pinpricks of light. It's so cool how this little junky, plain-looking thing holds so much beauty inside.

I get lost again in the ring, thinking about the stars that I'll maybe-but-probably-not get to ever see spread out above me in my dream future.

I'm interrupted by a tiny noise behind me, and my stranger-danger sense kicks in. I spin around, ready to either beat it fast or kick some ass, but all I see is a water bottled half-filled with some mystery brown stuff lying in the filthy gutter.

I shrug and walk on, but before I've taken a dozen steps, I hear it again. I whirl around again, and I swear I see a quick flash of movement slide around the corner of an old abandoned building and out of sight. I stand still and hold my breath, straining to hear the sound again.

Nothing.

And that's really freaky. Where the hell is everyone? I mean, I know it's hot out here, but is it really that hot? Has the sticky heat driven everyone inside today? I can almost always count on seeing at least a few dingy, half-naked, barefoot toddlers and their chain-smoking moms running around here. Not even Carla, Willow Landing's resident porch-sitting grandma, is out here today. Super odd.

I listen. A distant siren cuts through the air, but there's no sign of the *shuffle-scrape* noise I swear I heard before. It's probably nothing, but I feel chills creeping down my sweaty spine. I don't know. There's just something about the silent, abandoned street that totally gives me the feeling that something definitely isn't right.

Standing here like a scared little doofus isn't going to help me out, so I decide to move my tail and leave this place behind. What with my messed-up shoe, running probably isn't an option unless I want to scrape myself off of the hot pavement, so I start a pitiful little speed walk toward the main downtown drag. I usually avoid it because of the noise and stink from the zillion cars and trucks that constantly zoom through. But I'd gladly trade that for the eerie quiet of this place.

The apartment buildings lining both sides of the street stare at me with their silent windows and closed doors. They look like a bunch of scared, open-mouthed faces. As I stumble along, my broken shoe fills up with gravels and gunk again. This time I don't stop to dump it out. There's no way I'm spending an extra millisecond here among these silent watchers. I shiver and hug my bony arms tight across my chest.

I'm about a football field away from the rumble of Main Street when I hear the noise again, louder this time. *Shuffle-scrape, shuffle-scrape, shuffle-scrape.* Without stopping, I look over my shoulder.

My blood runs cold...

Chapter 17

ALL THE HEAT in the world vanishes, and I'm frozen on the spot. He comes at me like something crawling its way out of a nightmare. Scared little deer me stands and stares. My mind screams *"Run! Run you idiot!"* but my body is a fear-drenched lump.

I stand and gawk. He's this tall, scrawny, dirty-looking guy that I'm certain I've never seen around here before. He's got this weird-shaped head with a big lump thing on one side. What little hair he has is greasy and stringy and falls all around his head like the world's most disgusting waterfall. He holds that freaky head of his at a weird angle, and he's locked eyes with me. He's coming right for me with this awkward almost-limp, and he's staring at me. I see a terrifying hollowness in those bloodshot eyes. My mythical female danger senses kick in, and I have no doubt that this guy is major bad news.

And he's coming right toward me. He cracks this little half-smile and reveals a mouthful of rotten teeth. If I wasn't in nightmare mode right now, I'd vomit.

But I'm still so small, scared, frozen to the icy pavement. Alone. I glance around, hoping to catch sight of anyone else, anyone who could rush to my aid and rescue me from this guy who's done nothing but I'm sure wants to do terrible things. There are no faces in the windows, there are no passing cars, there are no friendly neighborhood superheroes.

I'm alone.

He comes closer, and his rotten smile widens. "Hey there,

pretty girl," he says in this croaky voice. It sounds like nails on a chalkboard. As he gets closer, my heart beats faster than I ever thought possible. I worry that it might break out of my ribs. He stops suddenly, and I see him reach down and pat his pockets with filthy hands. He's got black gunk under too-long fingernails. He wants to make sure he's got something, and his right hand settles on a long, thin lump in his right pocket.

He smiles again. He takes a step toward me. I finally come to my senses, turn tail, and run for it.

He follows.

The doors and windows of Willow Landing smudge together in a blur. The *shuffle-scrape* behind me quickens. I risk a glance back and feel a warm relief spread through my terrified body. Though he's running now, too, he's no match for me. He's falling behind.

I am the wind. I rush toward freedom, toward the busy street where there's sure to be someone, anyone to help. I look back again. He's even further behind now. I'm going to make it. Just a few more steps to safety. I'm going to be okay.

And just when I'm certain that I'm going to escape from this living nightmare, my stupid shoe catches on a crack in the sidewalk. The pavement rises to meet me, and I crash. Hard.

The rough concrete blasts the air out of my lungs. I gasp for air, desperate like a fish just yanked from the water. I lie dazed and paralyzed, my panicked brain commanding me to move my stupid tail before this creep is on me and does God-knows-what to me.

He laughs. It's this wheezy, "I'm about to do something evil" laugh straight from a horror flick. I flop onto my back and get into this half-sitting position. When I prop myself up on my hands, I feel a wet burning. If I make it through this, I'm going to need some new skin.

Before I know it, he's practically on me, and I'm seriously thinking that this is it for me. My legs flail like pool noodles as I try to scramble to my feet, but the ground turns to jelly under my shoes. My torn hands leave little streaks of blood on the pavement. A screaming panic runs through my body, but no screams, no words come out. I'm still gasping for breath.

Closer.

Mommies and daddies tuck their babies in tight and give them kisses and tell them that there are no monsters in the closet. Mommies and daddies say there's no such things as monsters. Mommies and daddies lie. Monsters are real, and this real-life monster has somehow crawled out of my nightmare and is going to gobble me whole with his rotten teeth.

He's here. He stops laughing and just smiles. He grins at me with his decaying mouth. I read hurt upon hurt in his empty eyes. He says nothing and reaches a bony hand into his pocket. I see his fingers curl around something. The diseased smile widens.

My heart is going to explode like dynamite and tear me into bloody ribbons. My mind is empty, erased by terror. I open my mouth to scream.

Nothing comes out except for a pitiful, small, squeaky voice. I manage to squeeze out a weak "No!" I'm a scared little mouse, and he's the bloodthirsty cat. Terror tears trickle down my cheeks.

My tears, my words have no effect. He reaches down for me with one hand and begins to draw the other out of his pocket. He's still silent, still smiling.

In the stories, the hero is always saved at the last second by some miracle plot twist. But the only plot twist right now is that there are no miracle plot twists. Just a bunch of awful, scary shit piled on top of even more awful, scary shit.

He grabs me by the hair. My scalp explodes into pain. The new hurt washes away some of the fear and awakens my body. He pulls harder and his other hand brings a thin, shiny something out of his pocket. The pain wakes me up.

"No!" I scream. And this time, my voice is loud and strong. It echoes off the buildings. He hesitates and loosens his grip. I kick out hard with my good shoe.

It connects with the soft between his legs. He howls in pain and falls to his knees. He grabs at his hurt. I scramble away and stand up. His howls turn to moans and I step back. I kick again, but this time, I add in all my weight and pain and fear and anger.

He wheezes out a rush of putrid breath as my foot hammers the place just below his ribs. This time, he's the one gasping for breath. He doubles over and topples onto his side, whimpering like a dog.

I turn and run.

This time, he doesn't follow.

Chapter 18

NIGHTMARE ALLEY FINALLY spits me out onto busy Main Street. Life out here rumbles on, people shuffle in and out of stores, honk and curse at each other in traffic, and trudge heads-down on the sidewalk, lost within their phone screens.

No one notices the filthy, bloody nothing stumbling along, shaking like a leaf in a thunderstorm.

All kinds of people pass me by as I stumble homeward. Most of them seem to go out of their way to not notice me. I just walk with my head down to make the whole charade easier for all of us. I've been avoided a lot by a lot of folks, so I'm pretty much used to it by now. I look up once and catch this lady and her little girl staring at me. When she sees my tear-red eyes and dirty face, her eyes widen and she pulls the girl closer to her. They sidle by me like I'm some poisonous snake.

They don't want an ugly, messed-up me staining their lives. I can't say that I blame them.

If I were some kind of a normal someone, would I want a *me* around?

I look around at this world of normals. Ugly Me feeds off of my fear and hurt and anger. She grows strong and takes over.

Ugly Me hates all of these people. Hates them because they aren't what I am. Hates them because they hold shopping bags and cell phones and smile as they walk down the street. Hates them because they walk by and don't have to care about this waste of air with dirty clothes and bloody hands. Hates them because they kiss their babies and cuddle their little ones and laugh and love and smile.

I thought for a second there that I could find someone to care that a girl just about got murdered or worse just one street over from their fancy stores and expensive restaurants. But I give up on that thought after the hundredth one pretends that I'm invisible. I thought for a second that someone would sweep me up and give a damn.

But I was wrong. So stupid.

I almost get smashed into a pulp by this big truck because I start to cross the street without bothering to look. He lays on his horn, one of those super loud air horns that smashes my ear drums, and yells out the window, "Watch what you're doing, dumbass!"

Ugly Me shoots him the bird and keeps walking. Maybe next time I'll get lucky and become a new stain on the pavement.

The adrenaline is starting to wear off. Little bits of pain begin to seep in and take over. I look down at my palms.

When I was a little kid, before Ugly Me came around, I had this pink princess bike. Dad used to take me to this old, abandoned church parking lot and let me ride.

I remember feeling like I could fly. I know now that I probably just crept along, slowed by tiny legs and cheap training wheels, but *man*, when I was on that thing, I felt so fast and strong. My bike was magic. I remember the breeze in my hair, the thrill of zipping around and around.

I was a race car driver. I was a dragon-riding queen. I was a jet pilot.

But most of all, I was happy. Dad was happy. He would watch and laugh and chase and we'd go home to Mom all sweaty and tired and totally in love with being an Us.

This one time, little daredevil me went a little too fast and took a hard turn. Thin plastic wheels were no match for what I was throwing down. One of them gave up the ghost, and I bit it hard. My little hands shredded on the pavement.

I cried and cried, but Dad scooped me up and carried me all the way home. He was strong and safe and warm and told me that being tough didn't mean never getting hurt. It meant taking the hurt and moving on and not giving up and getting stronger because of it.

At home, Mom cleaned my bloody little hands and gave me big doses of hugs and kisses. She put on medicine and pony Band-Aids and lots and lots of love. I fell asleep with them on the sofa all cuddled up warm with hurt hands but a whole heart.

I look down at my hands now. They look so much like those bloody little girl bike crash hands. Little stones and flecks of black are stuck in the red. I know it's going to hurt like hell cleaning all of those out.

But at the same time, they look nothing like my little girl hands. These are no longer little innocent hands like those were. These hands are mean, ugly things that have punched and slapped and done bad things.

I notice the ring again. It's all scuffed up now, and my blood has run into the scratches in its surface. It's stained and ruined, just like everything else in my life. I try to take it off to see if the stars are still there, but it hurts too bad to slide it over my cut finger.

It's probably for the best that I can't get it off now. I know the stars probably won't appear through the scars and the red, but as long as I don't look, I can still hold onto this microscopic shred of hope.

I walk toward home, my bloody hands hurting more with every step. I want more than anything right now to walk into my house and show Mom and have her coo over me and clean me up and cover me with Band-Aids and warmth and happy.

I want to tell her about Nightmare Man and watch her freak out and call the cops and hug me hug me hug me.

My tired feet climb the porch steps (always skipping the broken second one). I turn the doorknob and wince with the pain of it.

"Mom," I call out...

Chapter 19

BUT NO ONE comes running to my rescue. Instead, two grown men I don't even know are camped out on the sofa. One guy is slouched down with his dirty gym-shorted legs all man-spread out like he owns the place.

He's got his face buried in a familiar cracked cell phone. I give myself a quick pat-down. Nope. No phone. I left it by the sofa this morning. I feel like kicking myself.

He doesn't even look up from the screen. It's as if I'm some invisible nothing rather than the scared, hurt, angry kid that I am. I think about letting Ugly Me yell at the guy for being a nosy asshole or snatch the phone out of his hands, but I think better of it. Around here, Ugly Me has a tendency to get beat down in a hurry.

This guy has a bunch of nasty-looking homemade tattoos all down his neck and scrawny arms. Lots of skulls and barbed wire and weird symbols and stuff. He slides his thumb across the screen, and I notice that he's got "HATE" spelled out across his knuckles in nauseous greenish ink.

Yeah. This dude probably wouldn't be too intimidated by even my craziest crazy.

The other guy is this huge, dark-skinned dude. He's got this horrifying black neck beard and looks like he was dumped onto the sofa out of a giant bucket. He's just sitting there, staring off into the distance with blank eyes. He doesn't acknowledge that a girl with bloody hands just busted through the door, either.

I kind of shrink back and freeze like a little scared mouse. I'm not sure what I expected. I can't remember the last time I came home to a warm welcome. I don't live in one of those "Honey, I'm home!" houses where everyone gets welcome-back smiles and hugs.

Most days when I come home, I get more of a sense of, "Oh, It's *you* again." But I thought that maybe, just this once, things would be different.

Stupid me.

I edge around the mystery men. I'm tense and ready to spring at the first sign of, well, anything. I swear, if one of those guys makes a move toward me, I'm going to explode. But neither guy pays me the slightest bit of attention as I slide past and head toward Mom's room.

The door is closed, which is weird, and I give it some soft little pecks with the back of my bloody hand.

Nothing.

I knock again. There's still no answer, so I turn the knob. I wince again with the pain of it.

Mom is in the bed with Shane. Not, like, *in bed* in bed, but lying fully clothed on top of the stained sheets. They're both totally out of it, dead asleep. I try to wake her.

"Mom!" I shout.

Nothing.

"Mom!"I shout, louder this time.

Nothing.

"MOM!" I yell as loud as I can.

"Shut up!" yells one of the guys from the other room. I flinch like a scared puppy.

Still nothing.

I walk over and shake her.

Nothing.

I shake her harder.

Nothing.

Tears start forming in the corners of my eyes. I shake her so hard that the entire bed squeaks up and down.

Nothing.

I can see her breathing, so I know she's not dead. Why won't she wake up? I'm pretty sure I know why.

But I need her need her need her! I keep trying. I shake her, slap her, pull her hair.

Nothing.

I put my arm under the back of her neck and lift her up. Her limp head droops. I let her go, and she falls back.

Nothing.

I'm big ugly crying now. I give up and head to the bathroom. When I cross the hall, I look into the front room and see Tattoo Guy stand up, put my phone in his pocket, and walk out the door. I open my mouth to cry out, to yell, to burn this guy for being a filthy, rotten thief.

But I catch myself in time to stuff a sock in it. I like my teeth just fine where they are, thank you very much.

When I get to the bathroom, I close the door behind me. I pull aside the cracked mirror above the sink and ransack the little medicine cabinet, hoping to find something, anything, for my burning, bloody hands. There are a ton of empty orange pill bottles in here. As I search through the cabinet, my sore hands make an awkward mess of things. The pill bottles become hollow orange dominoes. One falls and takes a whole bunch of them down with it. They clatter all over the floor, making an awful racket.

That's me. An awkward mess, always screwing stuff up.

I do manage to get my hands on a half-full bottle of alcohol and a ratty old roll of gauze. That'll just have to do.

I twist the knob on the cold side of the faucet.

Nothing. Not a drop comes out.

I twist the knob on the hot side of the faucet.

Nothing. It's the Sahara over here, too.

I close the cabinet and thump my forehead against it. Mom was supposed to pay the water bill today. We got one of those scary "Last Notice" papers in the mail the other day, and I'd even stuck the damned thing on the fridge so she'd remember. Panic starts to rise up as I think of all the things I won't be able to do if there's no water. I shove it down for now.

I look down at my hands. If I don't clean them somehow, I just know I'll catch some zombie rotting flesh disease from the sweat and street gunk all pasted in with the blood and dead skin. No, thank you. I try the knobs again.

Nothing.

I look down at the bottle of alcohol. I'm not an idiot, but girl's gotta do what a girl's gotta do.

I brace myself and squirt it all over my right hand, blasting at the flecks of black gunk. I bite down on my lip to keep from screaming as invisible flames engulf my hand. My scrawny body starts to tremble.

I switch hands. No surprises here; it burns like hellfire, too. I bite my lip harder. I taste blood.

I try to wrap my hands with the gauze and make messy work of it. It figures. I was never any good at arts and crafts. I come out looking like a discount mummy crossed with one of those cage fighter guys--one of the crappy ones who get punched in the head too many times and winds up with brain damage.

I leave the bathroom looking like a crime scene with the sink streaked with tiny dirty rivers of blood and wadded-up pieces of gauze everywhere. The red and garbage blend in just fine with the rest of the decor around here. Mom has really cultivated a nice layer of nicotine-stained filth throughout the house.

My empty stomach makes its presence known with a loud, angry roar. I head to the kitchen. I'm not sure what I expected, but when I open the cupboard, I feel like screaming.

Chapter 20

NOTHING. THERE'S NOTHING there. The place has been picked clean today. Not that there was much here in the first place, though.

The fridge is empty except for a couple of cans of off-brand Coke and a jar mayo so old that it's probably become some kind of biohazard. I grab a can of the soda and crack it open. The *hiss-pop* makes me jump all Nervous Nellie a little bit.

The last time I drank one of Mom's sodas, I had to carry around a nasty bruise for a few days. When Mr. Gorley asked me about it, I made up some story about tripping over the dog and falling down the stairs.

But here's the thing: I don't have stairs or a dog. But I do have enough sense to know that snitching on my mom would lead to nothing but a buttload of trouble for us.

I lean against the counter and take a few sips. If Mom gets pissed about her Coke, I'll just lie and blame it on Neck Beard or Phone Thief. The Morality Police at school always talk about how honesty is always the best policy. That's easy for them to say. In my world, I wear lies to protect myself like those knights in the stories wear shiny armor.

I walk over to the hole in the wall and shove my hand inside to fish around for my crusty old cash. My mummified mitt barely fits, and just feeling around inside the wall and scraping it around hurts like a mother.

I grit my teeth and keep feeling around for it. After a miniature moment of panic, I'm relieved when my fingers eventually brush across the paper. I lift it out, barely hanging on like one of those quarter-sucking crane games at the store. By the time I get it out of there, poor Lincoln's face is all smeared with dirt and blood.

I pocket the cash and slip past Neck Beard again. Totally freaky. I hit the street and head toward. the dollar store. It isn't dark yet, so the corners and hidey holes in the parking lot shouldn't be overrun with shadowy people. Mom sent me to the store at ten o'clock one night because she said she needed a Mountain Dew, and I seriously thought I wasn't going to make it home alive because this one guy with too many facial piercings and not enough teeth followed me across the parking lot and kept asking me if I needed a daddy.

The store is just down the street, so it takes me no time to get there, even with my messed-up shoe tripping me all the way. As I walk along, the pain in my hands starts to ease up just a bit. You'd think that would be a good thing, but when my brain focuses on the pain in my body, it tends to forget about the pain in my heart.

What's wrong with me?

A punch to the face? No problemo. Easy-peasy. But that shattered, deflated look a grown-up gives you when you walk in the room and they obviously were praying that you skipped school again but here you are polluting their airspace so now "Oh great, *her* again" is written in big capital letters all over their face? *That* hurts like a mother.

Bruises fade in a few days, but those looks stick around and wreak havoc for a long, long time.

This one time in fifth grade, I missed, like, seven straight days of school because me and Mom had to skip town for a few days and hide out with this friend of hers. The whole time I was there, all I could think about was getting back to school. I missed my friends. I missed the warm. I missed the food that everyone else complained about. I missed the people that seemed to give a damn about me. I couldn't wait to go back.

She never told me what we were hiding from, but when we finally went back home, the place was trashed and a bunch of our stuff was gone.

I was so excited to finally go back to school, but when I walked in, I heard the lady behind the desk say to someone, "Wow. She's actually here today. Can you believe it?" Talk about feeling welcome.

I hear crap like that all the time. The grown-ups tell us that it's rude to talk about people behind their backs, but then you hear these upstanding role models talking mad-crazy crap about kids like me and about each other and about their bosses and everyone else. Trust me. I've spent a lot of time simmering in the school office. I've heard things. A lot of them.

They must think no one hears. But those words are megaphone loud and ugly mean.

After that, I walked into class still smiling big, and Mr. Sealy gave me *that* look. I shattered into a million little pieces of me.

I didn't come back to school after that until the principal came to my house and threatened to take me and Mom to court if I didn't start showing my face.

As the hurt leaves my hands, images of Headband Girl and Math Lady start to dance around in my head. The whispers, the eye rolls, the curled-lip "What's that smell?" looks, the impatient sighs all zoom and ping around behind my eyes like pinballs. They light up all the wrong bells and whistles, and the pain comes back hard.

Before I walk into the store, I slap a light pole. I leave behind a bloody smear. My hand explodes with delicious pain, and those ugly thoughts fade into the fiery background.

That's better.

Chapter 21

THE LADY BEHIND the counter is a vulture. She's this scrawny, leathery beast with a big nose and even bigger hair that she teases out into this totally 80's lady fro thing. She stays perched there with her long turkey neck looking around all hungry and waiting to pounce on the next piece of dead meat who decides to act like an ass in her store. She's got this killer smoker's voice and is constantly croaking at the feral kids and junkies who wander through the store in a constant flow of crazy.

I don't know how she does it. The people who come into this joint are animals who lie and cheat and try to steal anything not covered in a dozen anti-theft tags. I once saw her chase this huge, muscular dude out of the store with an umbrella after she caught him on her little camera monitor trying to lift some earbuds.

When I walk in, she turns and gives me the once-over. During this little visual pat-down, she gives my bloody, bandaged hands a little extra attention. She locks eyes with me and gives me this concerned look. I give her a little awkward wave and head past the cheapo cell phone accessory display and hightail it toward the pitiful little grocery section of the store.

Mom sends me in here a lot, so I pretty much know where everything is. That's a good thing because I don't like spending any more time in the back of the store than I need to. The shelves back here are tall and close together, and I get a serious case of the heebie-jeebies thinking about what could happen to me if some creep cornered me back here.

I grab for a pack of ramen, but I suddenly remember the old

H_2O situation back home. Damn. I'm going to have to get cup noodles, which are twice the price and have those gross little vegetable chunk thingies floating around in them. I nab an armful of them, snag a box of granola bars, and somehow manage to shove a big bottle of water into my armpit. I must look like a total dweeb. I head back to pay the bird.

I make it maybe three and a half steps before I trip over my stupid shoe and drop everything. Little white styrofoam noodle cups skitter across the floor. The water bottle rolls under the shelf with the dust and hair and mouse turds.

I'm not too sure what happened. The only logical thing I can think of is that there for a second, I must have felt just a little bit okay. And we all know that that can't happen, so the universe popped up and reminded me of my place in the big, bullshitty scheme of things.

Vulture Lady hears the ruckus and shuffles over to me. "Y'okay, hon?" she croaks. She bends over and starts helping me gather the debris.

"Yeah," I say. I reach my arm under the shelf and pull out the bottle. It's got crap all over it now. "Stupid shoe tripped me up." I nod down toward my shoe. The sole is almost completely ripped off at this point.

"Explains the hands, then," she says. I guess she's kind of right. Except for that whole part about the disgusting killer psycho, of course. Can't forget that.

"It's okay. My mom is getting me some new ones tomorrow," I say. Liar, liar, pants on fire. She would actually have to be awake and coherent to do that. Fat chance.

She walks with me toward the register. On the way, she grabs a roll of silver duct tape. She rips the plastic off of it and reaches out a leathery hand. "Gimme the shoe, hon. You could break your neck before then." I slip off my smelly, filthy shoe and hand it over. She jerks a long piece off of the roll, making that super satisfying duct tapey rip-stretch sound. She wraps it around my shoe a few times and hands it back to me.

I slip the shoe back on. I won't say it's as good as new, but it's a ton better than it was before. At least now I won't be a walking, tripping safety hazard. I smile up at Vulture Lady. "Thank you so much," I say.

"Don't mention it, hon," she says. She starts beeping my items through the scanner while I pull out my bloody Lincoln. The little screen shows that I owe her $5.62. Geez.

"Oh," I say, thinking fast of a lie to shield myself from the embarrassment of having to admit that I have a serious lack of cash. "Hold on. I don't think I need, um, all of those noodles. Lots of sodium, you know?" I grab for a couple of them.

She gives a little half-frown. She's not buying it. "Well look at that," she says, sounding like she just discovered a new species or something. "These two cups are dented. Can't sell 'em like that." She points to a couple of the cups on the conveyor belt.

"But I'm the one who--"

"Why don't you just take these? Going to have to throw them out otherwise." She doesn't wait for an answer. She bags them up and punches a few buttons on her keyboard. The new total of $4.85 pops up on the screen.

I don't say anything. I hand her my cash, and she gives me back a dime and a nickel. I slide them into my pocket, wincing with the pain of it. I grab my bag and head to the door.

"Thank you," I say, turning to look back at her. "Seriously."

She just gives a little smile and a nod. I turn around and open the door. The heat smacks me in the face.

"Wait a sec, hon!" I hear behind me. I turn around, and she drops the roll of duct tape into my bag. "Just in case," she says.

Chapter 22

WHEN I GET back home, things are still status quo. Meaning, of course, that things are still all screwed-up crazy. Weird dude on the sofa. Mom still passed out. No running water. Tons of leftover hurts.

It's going to be a long night.

I use the bottled water to fill a noodle cup up to the little line inside. I pop it into the microwave, which I know you're not supposed to do because of radiation and styrofoam chemicals and other sciencey things I don't know much about. It'll probably give me cancer in 20 years or something.

I don't really care, though. I have to somehow find a way to survive the seventh grade before I can worry about crap like that. Let's face it: at the rate I'm going, I'll be lucky to make it to Halloween.

I stand in the kitchen, one eye on the humming microwave and the other on Neck Beard. I'm almost used to the tide of random creepazoids that flow in and out of here, but that dude totally gives me the heebie-jeebies for some reason.

The bright *ding* of the microwave cuts through the quiet tension and makes me jump. It sounds oddly crisp and clean and stands out weird against all the ugly dull in the house.

Bright and happy things don't belong here anymore.

I take my noodles and sneak out to the front porch. Though it's still hot outside, the porch catches a little bit of a breeze. It's not totally miserable out here. I sit for a while and fork slimy noodles into my pie hole.

I slurp in silence. When I come across those gross, too-colorful fake veggies, I flick them into the trash-covered thing that passes as a front yard. Pretty soon, little brown birds arrive from nowhere and begin to scoop them up.

They seem pretty happy with themselves. They bob up and down with those little birdy hops as they peck around. One of them swallows an orange something and lets out this little twitter-giggle. Two more friends arrive and want in on the goods.

The little guy doesn't seem to mind that keeping his little birdy trap shut would mean more food for him. He just keeps yapping. More little birdy buddies join in.

I dig around my cup for more. When I've mined all the rejects, I open up a granola bar and start to crumble it into little bits. I begin to toss those out. When the birds start in on those little sweet nibbles, they lose their birdy minds and start to bounce and flap and talk all kinds of excited little birdy talk.

I watch. I start to throw the crumbs closer and closer to my stinky feet. Before long, they're all jumping around and chitchatting and being birdy happy on the porch right in front of me. It's kind of nice, really. I think about Mr. Science Teacher. He'd probably lose his crap right now. Maybe I'll tell him about it.

If he'll even bother to listen to me.

Everything's fine until this one bigger bird shows up. He's this pushy blue thing with a shrill voice who goes right to bullying the little ones. He hops around and flaps his wings and chases the little guys away from the food.

For a while, everything is chaos and feathers and little birdy curse words all around. Then a few of the little ones get the idea to band together and go after the jerk with a million little flaps and pecks. Once this happens, bully bird doesn't stick around. He jets it on out and doesn't come back.

That's what I need--a flock of plain little birds like me. We could hop through life looking out for each other. We could be happy being awkward and weird because no one would want to mess with us and crush our little birdy spirits.

But that's just the problem. I'm more like the shrill outcast with a serious lack of social skills. I'm the one that people drive away with their mouths flapping out those hurtwords and those mean looks pecking right into the soft flesh of my heart.

I think about Emmaline and Achilles and IBS. I look down at my damaged hand and finger the little plastic star ring. Do I dare to hope that I might have found my flock?

I don't think so.

Because I know that it's only a matter of time before Ugly Me shows herself. Then they'll run screaming all Red Rover, Red Rover to the other side and become just another set of mouths that gag on me and spit me out like I'm the disgusting hairball that I am.

How could they possibly understand?

I push that thought out and focus on the feast in front of me. We had this hummingbird feeder at our house when I was little. It was one of those pretty, dainty-looking glass deals that looks like an hourglass with arms. Dad brought it home and gave it to Mom one day. It made her smile that smile that made the room light up. She made this sweet red juice and filled it up and hung it from the porch ceiling.

We would all sit out there in the evenings listening to the tiny jet engine hums and buzzes as little emeralds with wings flitted around our heads. When they got close, we would laugh and smile, and I swear the little things were laughing and smiling right along with us.

When the bad times came and we became shattered, so did the red-filled feeder. Broken against the wall of our house, its shards were still in the yard when we moved out.

I never saw another hummingbird. I never saw another one of my mom's room-brightening smiles, either.

I taste warm, salty wet. When did I start crying? What is wrong with me?

Chapter 23

I WATCH THE birds flit and play while I ponder the meaning of my pitiful excuse for an existence until the sun starts to dip behind the downtown buildings in the distance. The day runs laps around and around my exhausted brain while the dark comes. Long shadows begin to take over my street and chase away my new birdy friends and the other daytime things. I resolve to spend the night out here because the thought of being even half asleep in a dark house with the guy on the sofa makes me want to vomit.

I survived my first day of seventh grade. I suppose that's something.

But I feel like I've been stumbling around in a briar patch all day. I'm scratched and cut all over--inside and out. Totally bloodied. I'll carry these cuts on my hands for a while, but the ugly looks and stinging words of the people who hate me for existing leave long-term scars too deep to see from the outside.

I'd kill for a shower right now. I'd love to wash this whole stinking day away and watch it swirl down the drain into black nothingness. But even if the water worked, there's no way to clean away the stench of those inside heart hurts.

Is there? Is there someone or something out there that can make me a new, squeaky-clean Happy Me?

I doubt it.

I look down at the now-damaged little plastic ring on my finger. I suddenly feel stupid again for getting my hopes up and letting myself believe in any kind of a future for myself.

For the millionth time today, warm tears form in my eyes. I grit my teeth and wrench the stupid ring off of my aching finger.

It hurts. A lot.

I cock my arm to toss the ring into the twilight. I don't need it. I know what's in store for me, and it doesn't involve any kind of happy nights under the stars.

But something stops me, keeps me from letting go. I hold the ring up and catch the last few rays of the evening sun.

The tears fall freely now, cutting tracks down my filthy cheeks.

Behind the scarred surface, through the filth and dried blood, I see the stars. They're not as bright as they once were, and there aren't as many, but they're there, calling to me.

I squeeze the ring in my hands and let the starshine fill me up.

I spend the rest of the night curled up in my chair on the porch, and in the morning, I step onto the bus. I'm exhausted, aching, and dirty.

But I'm going back. I'm going back because today has to be better than yesterday. Because if I don't, if I stay here, if I shut off now, then any hope for those starry skies will disappear into a long and dark nothing.

Want to find out what happens next?

Check out the sequel!

Available now on Amazon!

Want More?

Read the free prequel story!

Visit the link below for a free eBook and audiobook version!

https://www.jestamper.com/sign-up

Made in United States
North Haven, CT
03 March 2023

33477279R00050